HELP! I AM A PRISONER IN A TOOTHPASTE FACTORY

The neon sign fixed up by Ronnie's Dad – an electrical genius – in the bathroom said 'NOW CLEAN YOUR TEETH'. When Ronnie does so he gets another message: 'Help! I am a Prisoner in a Toothpaste Factory'.

Ronnie sets off on the toothpaste trail, desperately trying to evade the wicked clutches of the chemist, and when Mum and Dad are imprisoned in Glum's Toothpaste Factory, his mission becomes even more urgent ...

Jacket illustration by Rowan Barnes-Murphy

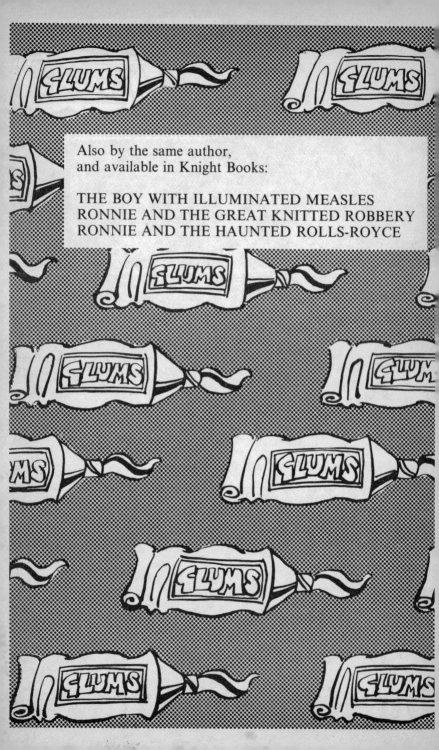

Also by the same author,
and available in Knight Books:

THE BOY WITH ILLUMINATED MEASLES
RONNIE AND THE GREAT KNITTED ROBBERY
RONNIE AND THE HAUNTED ROLLS-ROYCE

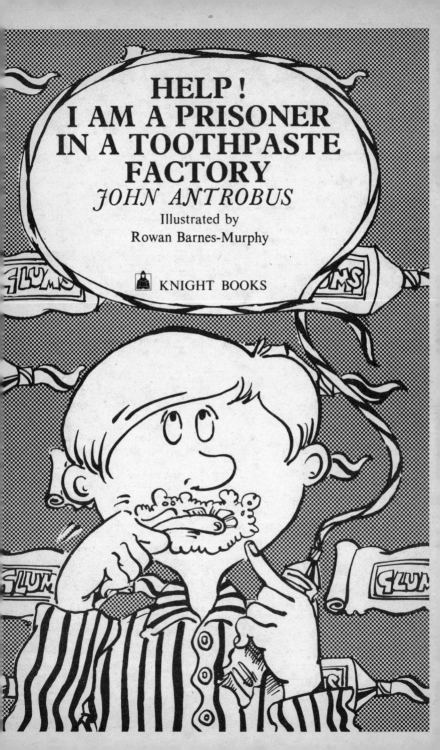

HELP! I AM A PRISONER IN A TOOTHPASTE FACTORY

JOHN ANTROBUS

Illustrated by
Rowan Barnes-Murphy

KNIGHT BOOKS

Copyright © 1978 John Antrobus
Illustrations copyright © 1978
Rowan Barnes-Murphy

First published in Great Britain in
1978 by Robson Books Ltd.

This edition first published by
Knight Books 1980
Sixth impression 1988

British Library C.I.P.

Antrobus, John
  Help! I am a prisoner in a
  toothpaste factory.
  I. Title
  823′.9′1J   PZ7.A634

  ISBN 0-340-25359-2

Printed and bound in Great Britain
for Hodder and Stoughton
Paperbacks, a division of Hodder
and Stoughton Ltd., Mill Road,
Dunton Green, Sevenoaks, Kent
TN13 2YA (Editorial Office: 47
Bedford Square, London WC1B
3DP) by Richard Clay Ltd.,
Bungay, Suffolk.

1

Ronnie was cleaning his teeth one morning. What a nuisance they are, he was thinking. Teeth are daft! Always needing cleaning—they're worse than shoes! Though shoes get muddy. At least teeth don't get muddy—not unless you start eating fields.

There was a sign in the bathroom, an electric neon affair, that usually flashed on and off like the ones in Piccadilly Circus. It lit up one letter after another, spelling out the message: "NOW CLEAN YOUR TEETH." Dad had fixed it up. He was a bit of an electrical genius. In fact he regarded himself as an inventor. "My boy," he would often say, "there's a fortune to be made in sitting right here." And then he'd add, "Don't think I'm asleep, Mother—I'm waiting for inspiration. It often comes in dreams."

For the time being, the "NOW CLEAN YOUR TEETH" sign was broken down—on Mum's orders. She had pulled the wires out. "That boy," she had

5

said, "standing up there watching that sign all day—he'll never get to school in the morning!"

Dad laughed and set fire to his newspaper. He wasn't one to let criticism get him down. "There's a fortune to be made in standing still," he said. "That's how the escalator was invented." Mum looked grim. Dad had installed an escalator in place of the old stairs, and she found it very inconvenient. It moved upwards for half the year, and then Dad reversed the machinery so that it moved downwards for the other six months. In any case it was now broken down, and Dad had moved on to other things.

Dad went on, "Why, even standing still we're travelling through space at an incredible rate! Running backwards wouldn't make that much difference, either!" He leaned forward. "Pass that tin of baked beans will you, dear? I'm going to conduct an experiment on it."

"Why? What are you going to do with it?"

"I'm going to eat it, and call it 'breakfast'."

Dad was tape recording all these early morning conversations—"for posterity. They'll begin to mean something by the year 2000," he explained.

In the bathroom, Ronnie stared at the broken sign, thinking how much he wanted his family to be happy. Just lately, Mum would go whole days without speaking to Dad—and Dad would give Ronnie messages for her, such as, "Where did you put my freshly-ironed shirt, dear?"

Mum would give Ronnie the answer: "It's not freshly ironed, and the cat's sitting on it." It was next-door's cat, and some days it would come in and sit on Dad's laundry.

"Well," said Dad, "if *I* lived with the people next door, *I'd* want to come in here and sit on my laundry! There's one thing for sure, I wouldn't go in there and sit on *their* laundry, I might fall through the holes!"

Ronnie laughed as he remembered the conversation. It was on one of Dad's tapes, recorded a few days ago, and he had played it last night while Mum was at Bingo. It could become a favourite, that one. The "cat" tape. It went on:

Dad: "That cat knows a good bit of laundry when it sees it! It's drawn to sit on my underwear by some strange, mysterious power. Like seeks like. It's good luck, having your shirt pressed by a cat sitting on it! Better than steam ironing. It doesn't get damp. Not unless you have a damp cat! The cat from next door's not damp. It's the only thing that isn't. See that patch on our wall? That's damp! That's from Mrs Pritchett next door. She's been leaning against it!"

7

Even Mum had had to laugh at that. Yes, there were good days and bad. All in all Ronnie would say he came from a happy family, though his parents didn't seem to be getting on as well these days as they used to.

Ronnie remembered the tape as though it had been recorded in his own brain:

Mum: "Why don't you chase the cat off your laundry?"

Dad: "There's too much chasing in this world!"

Mum: "You'll get whiskers all over your shirt . . ."

Dad: "Then I'll shave it!"

Mum: "When are you going to fix the damp patch on the wall?"

Dad: "I'd need to get Mrs Pritchett dried out first . . ."

"RONNIE! HURRY UP! You'll be late for school!"

That wasn't on the tape. That was Mum calling from downstairs.

"Goodbye, Ronnie! Farewell!" he heard Dad shout. "I'm off to work—for a bit of peace and quiet!"

The front door slammed.

Had he cleaned his teeth? Ronnie had forgotten. Better clean them again to make sure. He picked up the the tube of toothpaste and squeezed the contents out onto the bristles of his brush, and half way up the handle. Nothing unusual about that, he liked a good mouthful of paste. But as he lifted the brush to his mouth, he saw something written in the ribbon of the paste:

Ronnie stared at it. Was this a new make of tooth-paste? He was used to the ribboned variety, with his special flavour—but he had never had messages in it before! Play it cool, he thought, and making a quick decision he cleaned his teeth. He went downstairs.

"Mum," he said, trying to sound casual as he gathered up his school satchel, "I know a man who's a prisoner in a toothpaste factory."

"*I'm* a prisoner in this house," replied Mum. "Now hurry up and get to school."

"Where do they make toothpaste, exactly?" asked Ronnie.

Mum looked at him. "I gave up a career to have you," she said.

"Sorry," chirped Ronnie. "What were you going to be, Mum?"

"How should I know? I never had time to find out."

Ronnie puzzled on this. 'Well, Dad could stay at home, and you could go out to work." He thought this might be more fun.

"I'm not trained for anything!" exclaimed Mum.

"You could be a lion-tamer. Don't worry, Mum, I'll think of something. Leave it to me."

Mum kissed him. "I'm not saying that I'd rather not have had you."

"Thanks," said Ronnie. "Bye bye."

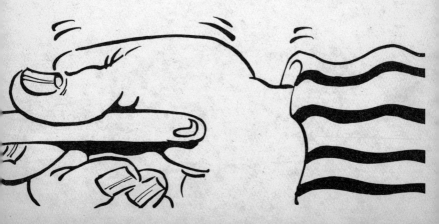

He knew Mum loved him. And, as he hurried to school, he decided he would find her a career. Maybe she could be a High Court Judge. Or a traffic warden. Anyway, he would look after her when he was older. And, until then, he would try and look after her while he was younger.

All day long Ronnie was thinking about the prisoner in the toothpaste factory. I bet he's not the only one, he thought. There must be lots more prisoners. He did badly in a Geography test, writing down that India was the capital of Paris. During the lesson he had drifted off in his thoughts, imagining Mum working as a lion-tamer in a circus—what fun it would be to visit her! Then it had got mixed up with the prisoner in the toothpaste factory and the geography of India. In Upper Bengal he and Mum were hunting for lions for her act, when they came upon a trail of toothpaste. Following it, they had suddenly been confronted by . . . the teacher!

"Ronnie! Wake up!" And he was back in the classroom.

After school, Ronnie sped homewards. His plan: to clean his teeth and see if there were any more messages. When he got home, Mum was waiting for him. She seemed more cheerful, and was reading a woman's magazine.

"Hello, Ronnie," she greeted him. "I've decided to make some cushions."

"Don't you want to be a lion-tamer now, then?" asked Ronnie, rather disappointed. "Mum, we *need* a bit of adventure in life. You'll soon get fed up, making those cushions—then you'll start throwing them round the room, shouting 'I'm bored, bored, bored!' "

"Nonsense," Mum replied, as she happily rummaged for material.

Ronnie was impatient to get upstairs. "I'll just go and clean my teeth," he said.

"Before tea?"

"Well, I didn't clean them the day before yesterday so I've got a bit of catching up to do."

He scooted up the escalator and into the bathroom. He needed more information. There had to be another message.

But the tube of toothpaste had vanished.

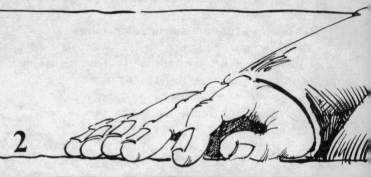

2

Mum said, "Dad came home early from work and cleaned his teeth."

"Did he use the rest of the tube up?"

"He must have done."

Was Dad getting messages, too? Why did he come home early from work? Just to clean his teeth? A likely story.

"It's your father's half day."

"All right—but he wouldn't spend all afternoon cleaning his teeth because he's got a half day off, would he, Mum?"

"What's the matter with you, Ronnie? Your father's gone to see Uncle Roger. They're building a new chicken shed."

"Did he take the toothpaste with him?"

"Of course he didn't."

Ronnie pondered this. A new chicken shed? Yes, his uncle did have chickens.

12

"But they built a new shed last month, Mum."

"Perhaps the chickens didn't like it."

"How can you tell if a chicken doesn't like its shed?"

"Ronnie, I don't know. I don't know anything about your uncle's chickens—and I don't want to know. Your father has a new electronic system worked out. When a chicken lays an egg a light goes on over your uncle's bed."

"Is he hungry?"

"What?"

"If he's that desperate for a boiled egg, you'd think he'd buy some from the shops, Mum." Ronnie didn't like the sound of that story at all. But further questioning was useless: Mum was already getting annoyed. And in any case, he had to go and buy some more toothpaste!

Mum gave him the money, glad to be rid of him for a little while, for she was engrossed in her cushion-making, and Ronnie set off for the chemist's.

As he entered the shop he saw the chemist looming behind the counter. So many boxes of pills, medicines and lotions were piled around that the light scarcely filtered through the window. In the gloom, the chemist, peering over the various displays—all in need of dusting—seemed stranded where he stood.

"Yeess?" inquired the chemist with a friendly leer that set Ronnie's hair on end, and would have had any dog barking immediately. "And what can I do for you, little boy?"

Ronnie did not like being called a little boy. "I want a large tube of toothpaste, please," he said.

"What sort?" asked the chemist, his smile devouring the scene.

Ronnie held onto the counter. "The sort with messages in."

"I don't know what you mean," replied the chemist, but his grin froze as though he had lockjaw.

Ronnie knew he could not trust the chemist. He might be helping to capture people and send them to the mysterious toothpaste factory, to make toothpaste all day.

"Would you mind shutting the door, little boy?" said the chemist.

"I'll shut it on the way out."

"Ohh, thank you." The chemist swayed forward as if caught in some sea breeze, and for a moment Ronnie thought he might topple over—capsize even. "Here is your mother's usual brand." The chemist plucked a tube of toothpaste from under the counter, thrusting it towards Ronnie.

Ronnie stared at him. "Are you sure?"

"I'm very sure. Very very sure." The chemist began to edge round the counter.

Ronnie quickly paid him. Fortunately he had the exact money, which he placed on the counter—not into the chemist's extended hand, that reached towards him like a bulldozer shovel.

'Don't go. I have some free sample cough sweets here."

"I don't have a free sample cough. Bye bye!"

Ronnie hurriedly left the shop. Down the road he stopped and took out his toothbrush, which he had brought with him to save time. He unscrewed the cap of the new tube, and squeezed out the paste. Yes! There was another message:

"HELP! THERE'S NOT MUCH TIME."

The chemist stood beside him. "You forgot your change, little boy."

"There wasn't any."

"Oh, yes—tuppence off on Thursdays. What are you doing?"

"Cleaning my teeth before they decay," said Ronnie, and shoved the brush into his mouth. "Toffees!"

"Toffees?"

"Toffees mean rapid tooth decay," Ronnie explained with his mouth full of toothpaste. "I always clean my teeth in the street if I've had a toffee."

"Very commendable. Come back inside the shop and rinse your mouth out. It's full of toothpaste."

"Good," said Ronnie.

"Good what?"

"Goodbye!" Ronnie ran down the street. As he turned the corner he glanced round and saw that the chemist was walking back to the shop. He slowed down. That was a close shave. He laughed. How could cleaning your teeth be a close shave? Still, he had put the chemist off the scent. What should he do next? He was probably the only person in the world who knew about the toothpaste factory, and the people who were imprisoned there.

"Dear God, what shall I do next?" he prayed. "Help me to rescue those poor prisoners. Amen. P.S. Thanks for the adventure."

Uncle Roger's house was nearby. Ronnie decided to call in and see him and his chickens. Perhaps Dad was still there. When he arrived at the small house where Uncle Roger lived on his own, the front door was shut, and nobody answered the bell. However, the side gate was unlocked and Ronnie went through into the small back-yard. The chicken coop stood open, but there were no chickens about. Strange. Uncle Roger always took the chickens on holiday with him, but this was not holiday time. Ronnie looked in the chicken house. Not a sign of a chicken, nor an egg. But pinned to the back of the shed was a note: "GONE TO BUY MORE TOOTHPASTE."

Why would Uncle Roger take his chickens with him when he went to buy more toothpaste? This was unusual, even for Uncle Roger. Things were definitely not as they should be. Ronnie went home.

Mum took the tube of toothpaste from him. "You've been squeezing it," she said. "You've been eating it."

"I can't deny it," replied Ronnie.

"What's the matter with you, Ronnie? Aren't you feeling well? Have you got tummy-ache?"

"No—I think the chemist is in the plot." Ronnie wanted Mum to understand. She could share this adventure. It would be good for her boredom—better than making cushions. "I'm going to watch out for the toothpaste lorry and follow it back to the factory— Mum, it's full of political prisoners! And Uncle Roger has gone to buy some more toothpaste with his chickens. That's not normal, Mum. Something must be up."

"Political prisoners? Uncle Roger's chickens? Oh, nonsense! What are you talking about?"

"I'll show you, Mum—then you'll believe me!" Ronnie grabbed the tube of toothpaste and started squeezing it all over the sideboard. "You'll see the messages, then you'll understand, Mum!"

But there were no messages on the sideboard. Just toothpaste. And an empty, squeezed-out tube.

"Go to bed, Ronnie." Mum was not unkind, but she could be firm.

So Ronnie went to bed, to await his father's home-coming. An explanation was called for. And Ronnie intended to ask a few questions himself.

3

That evening Dad sat on the end of Ronnie's bed.

"I've been getting messages in the toothpaste," declared Ronnie.

"Oh, is that right? Were there any for me?"

"They're from a prisoner, Dad. He's trapped in a toothpaste factory."

"I see. That can happen. I had a friend once who was a prisoner in a sausage factory."

"You mean he was locked in? He couldn't get out?"

"Oh, they didn't have to lock him in—he needed the money! It's what he *thought* that matters. You see, Ronnie, a person can be trapped and imprisoned by his own thoughts. That's why I am a free man."

Dad smiled. Ronnie knew his father had a wonderful spirit that roamed far away from the big store where he worked—"where my earthly remains are anchored," as he liked to say.

"Dad—where were you this afternoon?"

"Well, your Uncle Roger didn't appear to be in—which is hard to determine even if you're looking straight at him. So I took a stroll."

"Dad, Uncle Roger took his chickens with him when he went to buy a tube of toothpaste."

"Yes, well, he's been a bit nervous about those birds recently. Uncle Roger gets very broody at laying time." Dad stood up. "Goodnight, Ronnie. Don't forget to say your prayers. God bless you."

"Be careful, Dad. Something strange is happening round here."

"All right, Ronnie." Dad went downstairs.

Ronnie always kept his bedroom door slightly open, and later, from downstairs in the kitchen, he could hear the sound of an argument.

"You're too easy on that boy!"

"Easy does it—what's the hurry?"

"He imagines all sorts of things . . ."

"That's a gift . . ."

"He can't tell the difference anymore between dreams and reality."

"There's only a thin dividing line between them. After all, Edison dreamed of the electric light, and here we are sitting under it . . ."

This very substance shall dissolve in dreams, and dreams renew the substance . . . Had Ronnie read that somewhere? Or heard it? It's true, he thought, I do *sometimes* invent adventures and act them out, but not this time. The messages were real! The chemist was real! Ronnie had said his prayers, but tonight he wasn't sleepy. He was wide awake. Perhaps if he left home Mum and Dad would stop arguing about him. When he grew older, he wondered, who would leave home first? Mum, Dad or him? Perhaps they'd all leave home together. That would be fun.

It was no good, he could not sleep. He got up and

20

looked out of his bedroom window at the quiet street. There was not much traffic about. A lorry cruised past, and stopped under a lamppost. It was a toothpaste lorry. On the side of it was written:

"BUY GLUM'S TOOTHPASTE FOR BAD TEETH—STOP THEM GETTING WORSE WITH GLUM'S!"

What was the lorry doing outside his house? Glum's was the toothpaste that the family used—the one with the messages in. Had they come from the factory to capture him, too? Perhaps he knew too much. Though Ronnie felt he knew very little. Just that someone needed help.

He gazed down at the lorry. No one moved. Nothing moved. Then he heard his front door close, and Dad came out, carrying a suitcase. Oh no! He was leaving home again. Ronnie hoped it wasn't because they had rowed over him. Perhaps it was because of next-door's cat. Or possibly because of an argument about money, caused by Dad lighting his pipe with one of the unpaid bills. Well—Dad always came back. He usually went to stay with Uncle Roger, and his chickens.

"Come back, Dad!" Ronnie wanted to call out. "Tell her you're sorry!" But before he could open the window and shout after Dad, who was walking down the road, two men leapt out of the toothpaste lorry and jumped on his father. They put something over his mouth until he went unconscious, then they loaded him into the back of the lorry and threw his case in after him. They shut and bolted the lorry door.

Ronnie wrenched the window open. "HELP!" he tried to cry, but the word froze in his throat as the two men got into the lorry and drove off. "Oh, Dad!"

Ronnie ran downstairs. "Dad's been kidnapped by the toothpaste men!" he yelled.

"Sit down, Ronnie." Mum looked up from her

cushions. She was sitting amid a maze of patchwork materials, and seemed quite happy. "You've had a bad dream. Sit down, son."

"You never believe me! They've taken Dad away!" Ronnie burst into tears.

"There, there," said Mum, putting her arms round him. "It must have been something you ate."

"They put him in a big lorry! A Glum's lorry for bad teeth that don't get any worse!"

"Your father has gone to stay with Uncle Roger for a little while."

"They'll both be in that toothpaste factory, Mum— prisoners for life!"

"Where is the box the toothpaste came in?" asked Mum suddenly.

"Upstairs. I'll fetch it."

Ronnie tore up the escalator, grabbed the carton from the waste bin in the bathroom, and rushed down again. Already Mum had her coat on.

"Where are we going?" asked Ronnie breathlessly.

"To Glum's Toothpaste Factory," said Mum, with determination. "We'll settle this once and for all."

"Wait a minute. I'll put my clothes on."

"And I'll make a note of the address."

Ronnie sprinted back upstairs. In no time at all he had thrown his clothes on. This was some adventure! Good old Mum. She always turned up trumps in the end. He almost fell down the escalator in his haste.

"I'm ready, Mum! Let's go!" He burst into the kitchen. The back door was swinging open. Mum had vanished. The toothpaste carton was on the table. Ronnie picked it up, and stepped out into the night.

Why had she gone on ahead? And where had she gone? He stopped under a street light and examined the box. Yes—there was an address. He read it out: "In case of complaint, which there should not be, return toothpaste and any bad teeth to: Glum's Products, Glum Lane, Glumly, Glums—"

"Gums?" A voice spoke in the night.

"Yes," said Ronnie bravely, "Gums-on-Sea."

"There's no such place. It's a false address." A man stepped out of the darkness, tall, thin, and toothless. "They took all my teeth out," he said.

"Who did?"

"Them!" The man cringed, as if in the grip of some nameless terror. "They did. I tried . . . to change my brand, you see . . ." he stuttered.

"Who did? What brand?"

The man whimpered. "I had lovely choppers. I was so proud of them. My wife used to polish them every night."

"Were they false teeth?"

"No—that's the hell of it. She only married me for my teeth. They were like pearls. 'Harold,' she used to say, 'if you didn't have such lovely teeth, I'd leave you.' How can I go home now?"

"Who took your teeth out?" Ronnie wanted to know. "Was it—Glum's?"

"Ahhhh . . ." The man vanished into the night, as suddenly as he had appeared.

"Come back," shouted Ronnie, but he was all alone. He ventured down a dark alleyway which he was pretty sure the man had taken, and came out by the river. The embankment was lonely and deserted. He was a fair distance from home. Left or right, which way should he turn? Either way was very dark. Ronnie decided to go left, but as he turned, from the right—downriver—he heard a familiar sound. Chickens! It was definitely chickens. He turned towards the sound. The clucking grew louder. The moon gleamed for a moment on the river, and Ronnie saw an old houseboat. The sound was coming from there. A hatch opened, and Uncle Roger stepped out. In the moonlight he looked a mad sight. In the daylight he looked a mad sight. There wasn't that much difference.

4

Uncle Roger steered the houseboat to the river bank. "Welcome aboard," he said. "Jump on."

Ronnie jumped aboard.

"Now, would you like some cocoa?"

"Yes, please."

"So would I. Pity we haven't got any." Uncle Roger laughed, and squawked. "Sorry," he said, "spending too much time with the birds. I am," he continued, "a very frightened man. Not a frightened chicken. I am a very frightened man." He laughed again, and squawked. "Sorry," he said, "it takes a while to get used to human company. And you are human. Never forget that, Ronnie."

"Right, Uncle Roger," replied Ronnie.

"Right. Hard a cardboard! Nargle the kipper! And off we go . . ."

The boat drifted down the river. Uncle Roger steered, the chickens perched all about him on the wheel and compass.

"Where are we going?" asked Ronnie.

"A good question. The further the better. I've still got my teeth—that's the main thing."

"Were they going to take *your* teeth out as well?"

"I didn't stay to ask. Squawk. Pardon," said Uncle Roger. "You see, Ronnie—you know that corner shop?—I went down there for some toothpaste. I had a strange compulsion to buy Glum's again. I'd only tried it once, because it had tuppence off. But in the shop I decided to fight off the urge. No, I thought, I won't buy Glum's. Why should I? So I asked for another brand. And the chemist served me."

"But why did you take the chickens with you, Uncle Roger?"

"I needed their moral support. You see, Ronnie, I knew
I was in the presence of evil. Squawk. Pardon. I nearly
went back and apologised and bought three packets of
Glum. But the chickens weren't having any of it. They
had sensed the evil as well. Not one egg have they laid
since I bought that first tube of Glum's. I waited till
dusk, then came to my boat—we are emigrating to
Austria."

"Austria's inland," said Ronnie.

"Is it? Australia, then. But there is an unearthly
attraction about Glum's Products, Ronnie, which fills
me with dread. Even now I've half a mind to go back
to that chemist's shop and buy three boxes of Glum's
toothpaste—and fall on my knees and beg his forgive-
ness for even considering another brand."

"It must affect some people quicker than others," said Ronnie thoughtfully.

"You mean I have a congenital weakness for Glum's toothpaste?" asked Uncle Roger, miserably. A new thought struck him. "Ouch," he said, shaking his head, "Why, I could turn this boat round and search out that chemist, and ask him to let me spend the rest of my life making toothpaste for Glum's! Oh, the honour of it! The privilege! Let's turn back!"

"Keep going," Ronnie directed his uncle. So, it had come to this, he thought. Glum's toothpaste must contain some drug or chemical which kept the user coming back for more. He supposed that, being young, he was better able to resist the effects of those chemicals. But Uncle Roger was known to be a weak character. His dependence on the wicked toothpaste was a warning to everyone.

"I'm known as a weak character," muttered Uncle Roger. "Squawk. Pardon. Let me be a warning to everyone."

The small houseboat chugged quietly down the river towards the estuary. It was warm in the wheelhouse and the chickens dozed off. Ronnie dozed off, and Uncle Roger dozed off. The boat occasionally bumped into the river bank, but no great harm was done as they tacked towards the sea. At dawn Uncle Roger awoke, scratched his neck, and let out a loud "Cockadoodle-dooo!"

"Sorry," he said. "It will wear off. That's why you're so good for me, Ronnie—human contact. Always remember, you're not a chicken."

For a moment Ronnie could not remember whether they were looking for somebody, or somebody was looking for them. Perhaps it didn't matter. "Your destiny will find you, Ronnie," his Dad often told him.

"Now, if we had some ham we could have ham and eggs—if we had some eggs." Uncle Roger stared at the chickens, who scratched around a little guiltily. "The prime purpose of a chicken is to lay eggs. Always remember that, Ronnie."

"It's the chickens who should remember it," replied Ronnie, rubbing the sleep from his eyes.

"Take a turn on deck, lad."

"Have we *any* provisions, Uncle Roger?"

"We've plenty of grit for the chickens. And soon they'll be laying. Soon. Very soon." The chickens scratched round the wheelhouse as Uncle Roger fed them, throwing some oats on the floor from a bag.

Ronnie went on deck. The houseboat was festooned with flowers, shrubs and strange plants. How we'll get this lot to Australia, I don't know, he thought. The sky was lightening, and Ronnie looked up. Was that the moon rising? But how could it be—at dawn? A pale ball seemed to be growing on the horizon, and climbing into the sky. The sun had not appeared yet, and perhaps he was imagining things.

Uncle Roger came on deck. "Perhaps we'd better call into port and get some toothpaste," he said.

"Glum's?" asked Ronnie sternly.

Uncle Roger shuffled his feet. "Well," he said, "just a few tubes."

"No, Uncle Roger, you're in enough trouble with the chickens."

"Squawk. Squawk." Uncle Roger sniffed the sea air. "Ahh, it's a mizzen mast day, and there's herds of mackerel below in fathoms five. Let's go fishing—catch our breakfast."

They cast some lines over the side.

"I wonder how weak a character I'll be today," said Uncle Roger.

"Try to think positively," Ronnie advised him.

"I will. After all, being a weak character is a great improvement on being a strong chicken."

"You're heading in the right direction," Ronnie encouraged him.

"Australia!" Uncle Roger beamed. "My wife ran away to Australia. Or was it Wapping? She met a Madagascar seaman who turned her head with his curries."

"Do you want her back?"

"I didn't like her back. I didn't like her front very much either." Uncle Roger laughed. "No—that was years ago. I think we're divorced. I've got some papers somewhere—I believe I hung them on the wall in the chicken house."

Ronnie scanned the sky. No sign of that strange ball. Soon they had caught some mackerel, and Uncle Roger fried them. It was getting warmer out on deck. The sun was up. What a wonderful place to have breakfast.

"What time have you got to be at school?" enquired Uncle Roger.

"I don't think I'll be going today," said Ronnie.

"As soon as we get to Australia I shall fix you up with a school. There's nothing like a good education."

"Mum and Dad have gone missing."

"They'll turn up. If you lose something, look for something else." Uncle Roger went looking for his watering can. "The plants will have to be done with sea water today," he said.

The chickens came out on deck and arranged themselves in the morning sunshine. Ronnie was happy. He was sure something would turn up to save the day. It always did.

"Found it!" Uncle Roger emerged from behind a herbaceous border, holding aloft a needle and thread.

"You weren't looking for them," said Ronnie.

"That's what *they* thought. Now I'll look for my lawn mower. Ahh!" Uncle Roger stumbled over the watering can. "Got it!"

Ronnie laughed. Uncle Roger was fun—even if his character had been weakened by his wife running off some years ago.

"I'll never marry again," said Uncle Roger, lowering the watering can over the side. "Not unless I want another divorce. Of course," he reflected, as the can filled with water, "a man may *need* a divorce sometimes. In that case he would be wise to marry first . . ."

Suddenly the ball that Ronnie had spotted in the sky was hovering over them. It had appeared out of nowhere, seemingly, and hung about two hundred feet above them, spinning and shimmering in the sunlight. It was metal. Was it? It seemed like metal. It was more pear-shaped, he could see now, rather than like a ball. It was definitely not the moon. It was an unidentified flying object!

Ronnie felt an irresistible magnetic pull. Silently, the object drew Uncle Roger's boat towards it on a spout of water. Doors slid open in the underside of the spacecraft, and the houseboat, Ronnie, Uncle Roger and the chickens disappeared into it. The doors closed, as the water spout fell away, cascading back into the sea. The pear-shaped object hovered an instant—and vanished.

5

The houseboat nestled in the hatch of the spacecraft. Ronnie, Uncle Roger and the chickens were still on deck, getting accustomed to their new surroundings. A voice chimed out on a public address system: "Stand by for decontamination process." A fine spray filled the chamber, like a mist.

"I hope that doesn't upset the plants," said Uncle Roger. The chickens began pecking around as if nothing unusual was happening. The mist cleared, and a warmth enveloped them. "Oh, look, Ronnie—the hydrangeas are flowering!"

A door slid open above them in an upper gallery. The chemist stepped through, flanked by two beings crowned with antennae.

"Look, said Uncle Roger, "they've got two antennae sticking out of their heads. I wonder if they can get all the TV channels on those aerials."

"Aren't you frightened?" whispered Ronnie.

"Frightened? Should I be frightened? I didn't know that. My responses are often slow. It's because of my weak character."

The chemist surveyed the scene. "Hellooo, little boy," he said.

Ronnie didn't like being called a little boy.

"You forgot your tuppence off. Here it is." The chemist produced a coin, and held it up.

"That's a good bargain, that is," muttered Uncle

Roger, and called out, "I'll have three tubes, please! Glum's!"

"Ahh," said the chemist, "you refused when you had the chance—on Earth."

"I was worried about the chickens scratching up your shop, sir."

"You bought an alien brand," the chemist rebuked him, "made on Earth."

"You mean Glum's is not made on Earth?" Ronnie said quickly.

"I ask the questions round here, little boy." The chemist leered. "You—your Uncle Roger—and the creatures, follow me."

Ronnie, his uncle and the chickens proceeded up a stairway to the gallery.

"Have you got another branch in this area?" Uncle Roger wheedled ingratiatingly. "I'm right out of toothpaste, and Glum's is for me."

"You—shut up," the chemist snapped.

"Me? Shut up? Well, that's easier said than done, but I'll make an effort. Squawk. Pardon."

"Sssshh!" hissed Ronnie as they followed the chemist. "He doesn't like you, Uncle Roger."

"I'm trying to win him over with a few pleasantries."

"Silence!" commanded the chemist.

"Is golden," supplied Uncle Roger. "And a stitch in time saves nine—say all of us."

"We know how to deal with your sort," growled the chemist.

"You mean there are more like me? I thought I was unique in the utter weakness of my personality."

"KEEP QUIET!"

"I am keeping quiet. Sometimes I don't speak for days—you wouldn't like that. I think that's why my wife ran off with the Madagascar seaman."

They were walking down a corridor, which, curving gently, followed the contours of the craft. The chickens fluttered about, alighting on various persons—if the strangers with the antennae could be called persons. One of the chickens had taken perch on an antenna.

"I am getting interference," articulated the humanoid-type creature.

"Do you need a licence for those antennae?" asked Uncle Roger.

"I am not allowed to speak to you," uttered the humanoid.

"Nothing personal, I hope," quipped Uncle Roger. He seemed in remarkably good spirits.

"I know why you're so cheerful, Uncle Roger,"

whispered Ronnie. "It's because you think you can get hold of some more Glum's, isn't it? You know it's bad for you! There's a drug in it that forces you to keep going back for more."

"That saves you having to remember to put it on your shopping list," beamed Uncle Roger.

"How many times have we walked round this corridor?" the chemist asked, irritably.

"Three, sir," stated the humanoid.

"Why didn't you tell me? Blast your tentacles! All these doors look alike. Where is the Master?"

"Everywhere."

"I am the Presence of the spacecraft," a voice boomed. "What have you to report, Mister Chemist?"

"These are the two suspects who did not cooperate with the market survey, Your Most High Commodity." The chemist bowed his head reverently.

"I am Glum," boomed the voice.

The chemist and the humanoids began to chant:

"GLUM, GLUM,
To captivate Mum
Buy a tube today.
Clean your teeth—
It's our belief
With us you'll always stay!"

"Very good," said the voice of the Master, His Most High Commodity. "Take the prisoners to Dental Care."

An inner door in the corridor slid open. They went through it, and the door closed behind them. They were in a dental surgery.

"Right," said the dentist—another humanoid. "Let's have you in the chair, then."

Without hesitation, Ronnie jumped into the chair. He had been taught that dentists were nothing to be frightened of, and this one seemed friendly enough.

"Hello," said the dentist, "been using Glum?"

"Yes," said Ronnie bravely.

"Open wide. Oh, what nice teeth you've got."

"I don't eat many sweets, and I clean my teeth regularly," Ronnie replied.

"I can see that," the dentist said cheerfully. "Keep up the good work. Next!"

The chemist scowled. "You are very fortunate, little boy, that you did not try to change your brand." He turned to the dentist, and pointed at Uncle Roger. "Here is one who did."

"Oh," said the dentist. "Is he for the factory?"

"Yes," the chemist replied with great satisfaction. "But first you must destroy his personality by taking out all his teeth. The usual procedure."

Uncle Roger began scratching the floor, like one of his chickens. "There's no need to destroy my personality

—I haven't got one. I even think I'm a chicken on some days."

He leapt onto a desk, perched there, and crowed: "Cockadoodledooo!" The chickens clucked round him.

"He might be more useful as he is," observed the dentist.

"I am. I am. I'll do anything you want," Uncle Roger replied. "I will betray anybody. In fact, taking my teeth out might strengthen my personality. It couldn't possibly make it any worse."

"This man's character is utterly weak, and totally destroyed already," pronounced the dentist. "I would be wasting my time taking his teeth out."

"He might have some last vestige of resistance," the chemist argued.

"No," said Uncle Roger. "I long to work in your factory—it would be the greatest honour I could imagine."

"Next!" said the dentist. And Uncle Roger was out of the chair.

The voice boomed out again. The voice of His Most High Commodity Tuppence Off, thought Ronnie.

"We are under investigation! The Galactic Trade Commission is examining our product! Proceed with the utmost caution!"

"Blast!" said the chemist. "What we feared most! Why can't they mind their own business? Is there no such thing as inter-galactic free enterprise? It must be Venus! They've been complaining about us! They've got their own brand of toothpaste—Ventron—so they're trying to get us into trouble with the Galactic Trade Commission! Blast! Blast! Blast! And nasty frogs' eyes!"

"You are trying to take over the world with Glum," Ronnie accused the chemist.

"And what if we are?" the chemist snarled. "You

are all trying to take over each other! It's quite natural."

"What planet are you from?" demanded Ronnie, hoping to get all the facts while the chemist was upset and off his guard.

"Glumdonis! We are from another galaxy—we are a race of salesmen, ever seeking new markets—new horizons! Sell! Sell! Sell! Never mind the cost! We are super-salesmen gone mad! Mad! Mad!"

"But," interrupted Ronnie, "if your product is the best, you don't need to bully us into using it. Don't you believe in your own product?"

"Ahhh . . ." The chemist collapsed into the dentist's chair. "There's the rub," he moaned. "The rub? The rub?" He sat up. "Rub it on? Rub Glum on? A new approach? Rub it on something . . ." He slumped back into the chair.

"Open wide," said the dentist kindly.

The chemist opened his mouth.

"Yes—that's a nasty cavity . . ."

Leaving the chemist in the dentist's chair, Ronnie and Uncle Roger and the chickens were led back to the chamber in which their boat lay. They climbed back on board.

"Did you notice?" said Uncle Roger. "That chemist had two little holes in the top of his head. He's not human either."

Ronnie thought about this. "They've taken his

antennae away from him?"

"Yes." Uncle Roger nodded wisely. "I bet he hasn't been paying his licence money."

The floor of the chamber opened, and a water spout came up to meet them. The boat dropped gently onto it. The spout fell back to the ocean, and they fell back with it. The beautiful spinning spacecraft hovered over them, and then moved rapidly away. It vanished.

"Time to head for home," said Uncle Roger. "We'll give Australia a miss today."

It was late afternoon—but of which day, they could not be sure.

"The fight's not over," said Ronnie. "I've still got to find my Mum and Dad. I've still got to rescue the prisoners."

It was warm. Very warm. The coastline looked unfamiliar.

6

"India!" announced Uncle Roger. "All ashore!"

They had beached in a sandy cove, where unfamiliar trees stirred their leaves in a soft wave of welcome.

"How can you be sure it's India?" asked Ronnie.

"I've never been sure of anything," answered Uncle Roger, "but I've found that saying so often makes it so. Care for a mango?" He picked a luscious-looking ripe fruit from a tree.

"Mmmm," said Ronnie. "Delicious."

"They are mangoes, aren't they?" enquired Uncle Roger. "That would most likely make it India."

"What do mangoes taste like?" Ronnie was enjoying the fruit.

"They taste like the things you're eating."

"Then this must be India."

"Yes."

"Shall we have a swim?" asked Ronnie. "It's so warm."

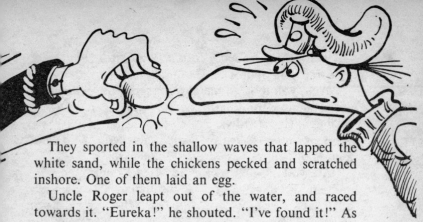

They sported in the shallow waves that lapped the white sand, while the chickens pecked and scratched inshore. One of them laid an egg.

Uncle Roger leapt out of the water, and raced towards it. "Eureka!" he shouted. "I've found it!" As he reached to grab the egg, a brown hand picked it up. An Indian looked over the sand dune.

"I confiscate this egg on behalf of the Indian Government," he stated.

"Why?"

"I confiscate everything on behalf of the Indian Government, that's why. Everything that comes ashore, that is. Customs and Exercise."

"Don't you mean 'Excise'?"

"I mean Exercise—they haven't issued me with a bicycle yet."

"That egg was laid ashore," Uncle Roger argued.

"Which came first, the chicken or the egg?"

"The chicken," said Uncle Roger.

"Then an age-old riddle is solved." The Indian gave Uncle Roger the egg. "What are you trying to smuggle ashore?"

"Nothing," replied Uncle Roger. "We were on our way to Australia. We got picked up by a spacecraft and given a lift part of the way."

"A likely story."

"It's the only one you're likely to get from us."

"Truth is stranger than fiction," observed the Indian. "My name is Singis Thing. I used to work in a laundry. I singed everything. Now I am a customs officer. Free uniform and boots! Sign here!"

Uncle Roger signed a form. "Why am I signing for your uniform and boots?"

"Well, you look to me like a responsible person."

"Is there a toothpaste factory round here?" asked Ronnie, determinedly.

Singis Thing looked suddenly frightened. "That's not a good question to ask around these parts."

"Are you a Glum user?" persisted Ronnie.

"Glum? Glum? Yes . . ." the Indian looked miserable. "It's sweeping our continent. Who will rid us of this curse?"

"I will," said Ronnie firmly.

"Where can I get some?" asked Uncle Roger.

"No, Uncle Roger, you don't need it."

"Don't I?" Uncle Roger looked dejected.

"I've got some here!" Singis Thing produced a tube of Glum's toothpaste. "Shall we clean our teeth immediately?"

Ronnie grabbed the tube, raced to the water's edge, and threw it far out into the ocean. When he turned back, it was dark. He saw his uncle and Singis Thing fading into the night. He ran up the beach. Stopped. Put out his hand—and touched a mango tree.

They've gone to get more toothpaste, he thought. He heard a faint clucking in the distance. That could be Uncle Roger—or the chickens. He set off after them. A pale moon came up, and soon he was able to see a little more clearly. He thought over the problem. True, Glum Products were in trouble with the Galactic Trade Com-

mission—but this might make them all the more determined to dominate Earth. And how many other planets were they planning to take over with their abominable toothpaste? They might even take over the Galactic Trade Commission. Ronnie's task seemed immense.

"Dear God," he said, "please help me find Mum and Dad, and rescue the prisoners in the toothpaste factory."

The stars came out, and winked at him, and Ronnie felt less lonely. He stopped, and listened. He could no longer hear the clucking of Uncle Roger, or the chickens. He was lost.

An orange ball appeared overhead. It was not the spacecraft he had been in before, nor was it the moon. That was up already. The ball grew bigger and bigger— or was it coming closer?

A voice echoed from the heavens: "This is the Galactic Trade Commission. We are beaming you aboard. Stand by!"

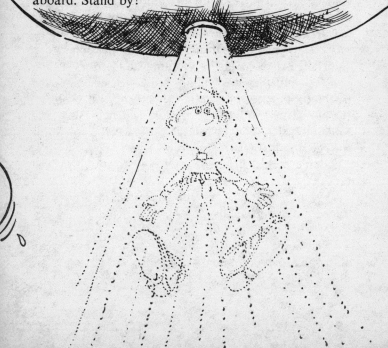

In a trice, Ronnie felt himself disintegrating. It was a lovely feeling, like when he was ill once, and seemed to be floating away from his body. He was not worried, only curious about what was going on.

He came to in a room of golden metal. A benevolent-looking creature—with three antennae—was sitting behind a desk. "Hello," he said. "Welcome, Ronnie. We are looking into some complaints we've had about Glum Products. Now, we need some evidence against them, and we think you can provide it. However, whatever decision we make must be fair and impartial and based upon the facts available to us."

"They're taking everybody's teeth out," said Ronnie.

"True—but this could be viewed as a kindly act of dental hygiene. We need something more substantial in the way of evidence."

"People are frightened."

"That's not enough. Sometimes people are frightened of good things, because they cannot understand them. On the other hand, they are often not frightened of bad things, because of their ignorance. Really they should fear less and less as they gain in wisdom. But it's a long process," sighed the Galactic Trade Commissioner.

"There are prisoners in a toothpaste factory."

"Yes—but they are willing, most of them; addicted to the toothpaste, but willing. It's a difficult problem. It's a matter of the balance of evidence. We need something else. You are a bright boy. Maybe you know enough about this business to be able to help us."

Ronnie racked his brains. Of course—the breakfast tapes!

"My father has tape-recorded our breakfast conversations," he said excitedly.

"Most interesting, but—"

"The point is, sir, that recently there has been a lot of trouble in our family—ever since we started using

Glum's toothpaste. Arguments. Some of them are funny, but these last few weeks Mum and Dad haven't been getting on at all like they used to do." That must be it, he thought. It's that rotten Glum's toothpaste.

"Let's beam the tapes up," suggested the Commissioner.

They went to a strange-looking machine, and the Commissioner showed Ronnie a screen on which they could pinpoint any place in the world.

"Yes—that's my house!" Ronnie pointed as they focused on his district.

"Right," said the Commissioner, "I will now demonstrate my powers of telekinesis."

"What's that?" asked Ronnie.

"I'll show you. It's moving objects through space using the power of the mind. Stand back now." The Commissioner went into a trance. The central antennae on his forehead began to vibrate. "I use no machinery," he said. "I've got past that stage. I am a black belt telekinesis expert."

Suddenly the tapes appeared in the room.

"Right—let's put them on the machine."

They could not help laughing as they listened to the tapes—especially that 'cat' tape.

"This should do the trick," said the Commissioner, looking suddenly serious. "These provide definite evidence of family disturbance caused by Glum Products. This could well swing the balance of evidence with the Galactic Trade Commission." He stood up, and extended his hand. "Thank you, Ronnie," he said. "Can we drop you off anywhere?"

"I must get to the toothpaste factory," Ronnie answered. "There are people in trouble there."

"I'm afraid we can't act upon that until we get a firm decision from the Commission. But I can beam you down anywhere you like."

"The toothpaste factory, please," said Ronnie.

"That's in Upper Bengal. We put the thought into your head during your Geography lesson—remember?"

"You shouldn't go round putting thoughts into people's heads," Ronnie reproved him.

"Sorry—but you were already inclined that way or we couldn't have done it. Farewell, Ronnie. Good hunting!"

Ronnie felt himself disintegrating again, that same strange sensation of being disconnected from everything, and yet having a lively interest in it all.

He came to on a mountain plateau. It was cold. He looked up and saw the orange ball, distant now. It seemed to rock, as if waving goodbye, and disappeared.

He was on his own again. But once more he could hear the sound of chickens. He began to make his way towards some lights that beckoned him across the plateau.

7

As Ronnie approached the lights, they disappeared, seeming to sink into the ground. The plateau was surrounded by mountain peaks. Ice glinted white as the moonlight reflected from the heights. Ronnie shivered. The air was so fresh and cold he felt he could touch it— swim in it—float on it. He took a deep breath, and felt better. A peal of laughter made him spin on his heels. Under a tree, the only tree for miles, sat an old, old man, squatting on the ground and rocking with laughter.

"Why are you laughing?" asked Ronnie.

"Once you start laughing, you see the funny side of things." The old man pealed with laughter again. "It's wonderful. You should try it."

"I like to hear a good joke first," explained Ronnie.

"Oh, well, in that case, how about this one: There was an Englishman, an Irishman and a Scotsman!" He clutched his stomach with laughter.

"Is that all?" said Ronnie.

"Oh, yes—that's the funniest one I know."

Ronnie sat down beside him. The old man's skin was as cold as the icy peaks. "Who are you?" asked Ronnie.

"I am a yogi."

"What is that?"

"I was hoping you might be able to tell me. I've spent my lifetime trying to find out. I am trying to reunite my soul with the Universal Spirit. But it's only when I stop trying that it starts to work."

Ronnie shivered with the cold.

The yogi's skin began to radiate heat, like an electric fire. He laughed. "There," he said, "that is warmer for you. That will be three rupees, please. Put it into my Bombay account." He burst out laughing again.

"I don't have any money," said Ronnie.

"Then you must learn to warm yourself. Think of the desert heat, and the scorching sun, and the blistering sand."

Soon Ronnie was sweating. He thought of taking his jumper off.

"That's enough!" cried the yogi. "Now, what can I do for you?"

"Can you tell me where to find the toothpaste factory?"

"It is in your mind, and will materialise in the fullness of time. You were born for adventure, Ronnie. Therefore adventure must come your way."

"Can you help me to defeat Glum's toothpaste?" asked Ronnie, earnestly.

"Well, Ronnie, there are two sides to the problem: there is the toothpaste, and there is people's desire for the toothpaste. Take away people's desire for Glum's toothpaste, and the market will collapse. But, as most people are not yet ready for that, you had better concentrate on removing the toothpaste." The old man roared with laughter, and began to float in the air. "I must go now, Ronnie. It has been a great pleasure meeting you." He hovered in the air, about three feet above the ground, still in the sitting position. "Good luck with your search. Don't forget to see the funny side of things. And above all—oh!—I *am* above all—"

The yogi floated away on a peal of laughter. He seemed to merge into the mountain tops, and become one with those snowy wastes.

And there was the factory! How could Ronnie have missed it? Right in front of him, only a hundred yards away. He ran towards it. A fence of barbed wire confronted him, lit by searchlights. Shadowy figures wearily lifted objects and hauled trucks beyond the glare round the perimeter fence. How was he to get in?

Hands grabbed him. Getting in was not going to be a problem.

The chemist leered as Ronnie was pushed into his office. He looked different ... then Ronnie realised that the teeth in his terrible smile were missing.

"Hellooo, little boy."

Ronnie did not like being called a little boy. "Where are my Mum and Dad?" he demanded.

"All in good time. First—how dare you try to disrupt our plans!"

"Who took your teeth out?" asked Ronnie.

"Yes—I have been disgraced, and must work my way back into favour, and get a lovely set of false choppers. However ... and another thing ..." The chemist seemed vague and bemused. "Yes ..."

"Yes what?" Ronnie asked doggedly.

"You have been the cause of my downfall. But it is merely a temporary setback. A successful sales campaign here on Earth will mean my promotion to Head Office on Glumdonis—with fitted carpet, my own desk, and central heating! Who could ask for more?" His eyes narrowed. "What did you tell the Galactic Trade Commission? I fear you have been in contact with them. But it won't work. We are a large company. We have influence in the galaxy, beyond your wildest dreams. Our shareholders stretch to the far reaches—" He waved his hand as though to indicate immeasurable distances, and knocked over a couple of humanoids.

"You cannot bring down such an empire with a mere complaint from a user—a wretched *consumer*. You are the smallest cog in our vast sales campaign."

"The consumer is the most important consideration in any sales campaign," said Ronnie, bravely.

"Ahhh!" The chemist reached towards him, but restrained himself. "No—we have a better idea for you —what is it? I'll think of it in a minute."

The chemist was running out of steam, Ronnie was sure of it. It must be something to do with the fact that his teeth had been removed. Yet Ronnie sensed that the man could still be dangerous. The chemist's voice interrupted his thoughts.

"Yesss, little boy, I will show you the extent of my power." He turned to the humanoids that guarded the room. "Bring her in!"

A door opened, and Mum was brought in.

"Oh Mum!"

Mum stared at Ronnie. "I am a Glum Mum now, Ronnie," she said monotonously. "I put Glum products first—before my family—before everything. I use Glum's toothpaste, Glum's floor polish, Glum's sink cleaner, Glum's shoe polish, Glum's hand-cream,

Glum's nail varnish, Glum's—"

"That's enough," said the chemist, with great satisfaction, rubbing his hands till they steamed. "Now, come with us, Ronnie, and see how our little factory works."

Escorted by the humanoids, they went out of the office.

"Never mind, Mum," said Ronnie comfortingly.

"I don't mind, Ronnie," said Mum, dully.

In the cold air outside, Ronnie thought he could hear a peal of laughter. The yogi? How could he laugh at such a situation? Then Ronnie remembered: "Don't forget to see the funny side of things." He took great heart, as he breathed in deeply. The darkest hour was always before the dawn. And soon the night sky would lighten.

They found Uncle Roger pushing a big truck, the chickens perched atop it.

"Hello, Ronnie," he said cheerfully. "Isn't it wonderful! All the toothpaste I can eat! Squawk! Pardon." He took out a tube of toothpaste and squeezed some into his mouth. He put the cap back on carefully. "By golly, that was good!"

He hadn't even used a toothbrush! Had Uncle Roger come to that?

"Where is your egg?" asked Ronnie, hoping to stir his uncle into some kind of rebellion. "Did they take it away from you? You know how long you waited for your chickens to lay—doesn't that egg mean anything to you any more?"

Momentary panic flitted across Uncle Roger's face. "My egg? They took it! But they gave me Glum's toothpaste. My egg? The egg? Yes . . . who's sitting on it? Are any of you birds sitting on the egg? No—they took it . . ."

The chickens looked at Uncle Roger as if to say, "We lay the eggs. It's up to you to look after them."

"Don't look at me like that!" Uncle Roger picked up a stone and aimed it at the chickens. "What am I doing?" He threw the stone down and said to Ronnie, miserably, "Why did you come here? You're spoiling the fun." He took another squeeze of toothpaste, and pushed the truck away, a bowed and broken figure.

"Now," said the chemist, "little boy." He rocked with power, and swayed with glory. "I will show you your father. Follow me." His eyes protruded with anticipation, and he blinked hard to get them back in their sockets.

"Father? Father who?" asked Mum, tonelessly.

"Your husband."

"I don't mind so long as I've got Glum," said Mum.

"Good, good. This way." The chemist rubbed his hands together so hard that they began to smoulder. He shook them and blew on them. "Ouch, mustn't do that."

He led them into a long shed, where a truly miserable sight met Ronnie's eyes. Crumpled grey figures attended incredible machines that ticked, rocked, shook and roared as they churned out endless Glum products. Occasionally a prisoner would reach into his pocket for a nip of toothpaste, and a spark of life would seem to tremble through his forlorn body.

"Atttention!" ordered a humanoid.

All the prisoners stood to attention beside their machines, and recited:

"Glum, Glum,
Oh what fun,
It answers all our needs.
Glum, Glum,
By the ton,
On it our whole life feeds.
Glum, Glum,
Here we come,
We are but shaken reeds,
Glum, Glum,
We poor scum
Are here to do your deeds.
Glum, Glum, we love you so,
Never ever let us go.
GLUM!"

The last word was shouted.

"Isn't it beautiful?" exclaimed the chemist. "Composed by one of our prisoners."

"Uncle Roger?" asked Ronnie, suspiciously.

"Yes—in gratitude to us for looking after his egg. We have it safe in our safe! But come. This way . . ."

Down the end of the shed, behind a huge vat, they found Dad. He still had his teeth in.

"They let me keep them so that my pipe wouldn't fall out of my mouth," explained Dad. "Yes, it's a grand life here. I'm a free man, and I choose—what's the word, now?"

"*Glum's*," said the chemist threateningly. "And if you want to keep those teeth, you'd better remember it.'

"Sorry, your honour." Dad bent down over the vat, stirring the toothpaste mixture in it.

"Soon you'll be happy, too, Ronnie," the chemist said with silky menace. "So how can the Galactic Trade Commission close us down?"

"The Trade Commission will make a fair decision."

"We provide what the people want," the chemist snarled.

"Yes—but the Trade Commissioner knows how you get people to want it."

"Get to work! You'll soon be happy here. You will be our first happy family working here. That will convince everyone."

"Yes," said Mum, "you'll soon be happy here—like us, Ronnie. We've never had it so good." She stared vacantly ahead.

"Mum—can't you remember what it was like to be *really* happy?"

Suddenly the roof shook. The building trembled.

"This is the Galactic Trade Commission," a voice boomed. "We have a ruling on Glum's Products."

At last, thought Ronnie, and only just in time.

"We find there is not enough evidence against Glum Products to discontinue their production. That is all. Roger and out."

"What?" said Uncle Roger. "Roger's going where?"

Ronnie felt an overwhelming disappointment. How could the Trade Commission make such a bad decision? He heard laughter. It was the yogi.

"How can you laugh, *now*?" shouted Ronnie towards the roof, where he imagined the laughter was coming from.

The yogi appeared, hovering near the ceiling, still in the sitting position.

"Ronnie, what is wrong with you? Fear not. Laugh. Laugh as if your life depended on it. Try and see the funny side."

The yogi disappeared. Had anyone else seen him? Ronnie didn't know. He looked at the dismal scene. What was there to laugh about? At that moment Uncle Roger staggered towards them, pushing the heavy truck. The chickens were pecking about cheerfully, and two of them were perched on his head and shoulders. He came up to the chemist.

"Do you think if I am very good, I could have a look at my egg—every Saturday afternoon?" he asked meekly. "Or if I'm asking too much, could I at least write to it every Christmas?"

Dad began to laugh.

"Dear egg," raved on Uncle Roger, composing the letter in his addled mind, "it would be nice if you could visit us this year, but it's the sort of trip that takes a lot of planning. Once out of your shell there's no going back—but that's life, for all of us."

Even Mum was laughing now.

"What are you laughing at? You are not supposed to laugh here!" growled the chemist.

Uncle Roger started to laugh.

"What are you laughing at?" barked the chemist.

"I don't know, sir. I'm only laughing because other people are laughing. It's my weak character."

The chickens clucked sympathetically.

"Cockadoodledoooooo!" screeched Uncle Roger. "An egg! An egg! My kingdom for an egg!"

The rest of the prisoners began to laugh. Suddenly, Mum pushed the chemist into the vat of toothpaste. He looked so funny, floundering in the ribboned mixture, they howled with laughter. Hoots of joy raised the roof, and the yogi's peals of mirth could be heard, ringing amongst them.

60

Outside, in the dawn sky, the orange spacecraft of the Galactic Trade Commission hesitated. Inside the craft, the Trade Commissioner hurried to the scanning machine. "What is it?" he enquired.

"We are getting interference," said one of his crew.

"A Galactic Trade Commission ruling is nothing to laugh about," said the commissioner. "I don't know though..." On the scanner screen he could see the inside of the shed, and everyone doubled up with laughter, rolling about on the floor.

"There is a message for you, sir," said another member of the crew, handing him a slip of paper. The Commissioner read it out. "Overlooked the tapes. Have just played them: plenty of laughs, but they show definite signs of disruption of family life by Glum's Products. Trade Commission ruling reversed."

"Well," said the Commissioner, "that's that." He looked at the scanner again, in time to see the chemist disappear beneath the ribboned muck. "They took the law into their own hands. They did not agree with our decision. Earth people have minds of their own. I am glad the decision in their favour came late—or they might not have known they had the power within themselves to begin putting things right."

The scanner moved to include Uncle Roger and the chickens. The Commissioner burst out laughing. "Oh, no! That's too much!" He doubled up, clutching his sides. "Make arrangements," he spluttered, "to have the factory blown up. Ha ha haha hahaha!" The Commissioner staggered back to the scanner. "Keep tuned in to Uncle Roger," he said, gasping for breath.

They watched Uncle Roger rush to the main office and force open the safe amidst a flurry of chickens and laughing prisoners. The egg shell lay in pieces.

A tiny chick jumped out, and perched on Uncle Roger's hand. His eyes filled with tears.

Transportation was arranged, and soon all the prisoners had been beamed back to their homes. Some had brand new sets of false teeth. Glum's toothpaste quickly disappeared off the market. The old chemist's shop was pulled down, and a parking lot was put in its place.

"There's progress for you, Ronnie," said Dad as they were taking a walk past the site. "Have you heard from Uncle Roger recently?"

"He's decided to stay in India, Dad. He's met a yogi, a wise man who's helping him."

"What—to be a stronger character?"

"No, to look after the chickens. They like it there. They're laying lots of eggs."

They went home. Mum was making cushions. Dad kissed her lightly on the cheek. "You haven't done that for ages, dear," she said.

"Well," said Dad, "I've been working a lot of over-time lately—at the factory."

When Ronnie went to bed that night, he prayed hard, thanking God for a wonderful adventure. "Dear God," he said, "if Mum gets bored again, we might need another one."

He heard laughter. And for a moment he felt the coolness of the mountains. He breathed deeply, and it was the air, crisp and fine, of the Bengal plateau. Ronnie fell asleep.